Chef Monty's Baking Rules

A happy baker bakes a happy pie.

Concentrate on what you're doing—no matter what.

If something unexpected happens, fix it as best as you can.

Always leave your kitchen the way you found it.

Don't give up, even when what you're making doesn't look the way it's supposed to.

A baker can always use a little help.

Always finish what you start.

A pie is ready when it's ready, and not one minute before.

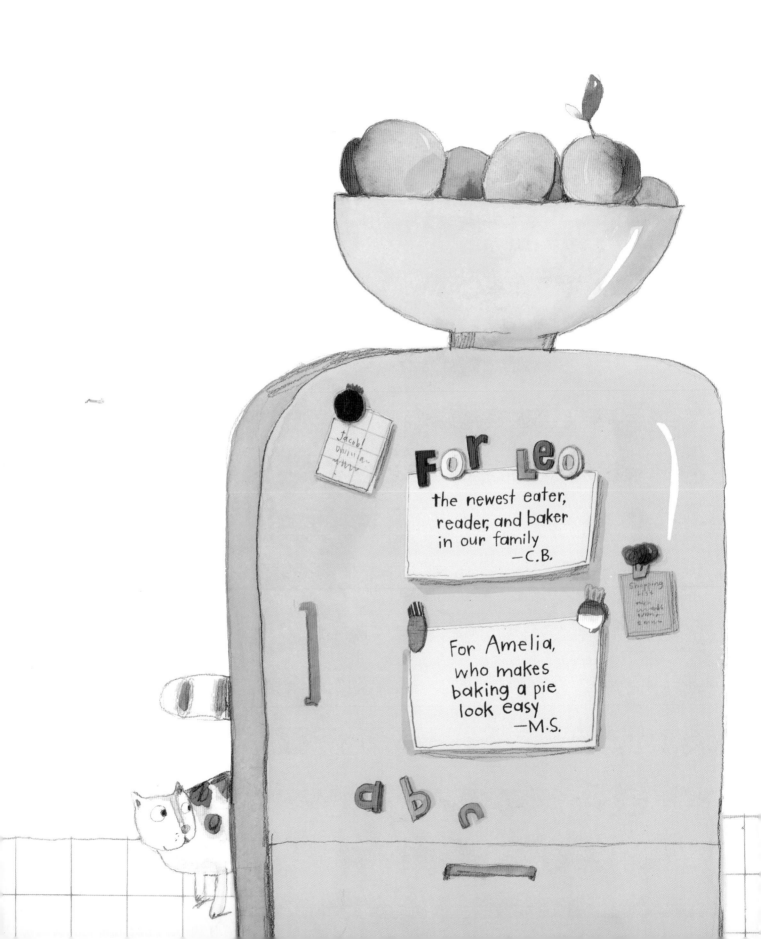

For Leo
the newest eater,
reader, and baker
in our family
—C.B.

For Amelia,
who makes
baking a pie
look easy
—M.S.

EASY AS PIE

Cari Best

Pictures by
Melissa Sweet

NOW YOU'RE BAKING!

Farrar Straus Giroux

New York

At the end of a long, hard day of school, Jacob sat down to watch his favorite TV show, *Baking with Chef Monty.*

"Baking is as easy as pie," said Chef Monty, "once you know the rules."

"I know the rules," said Jacob, who had seen the show a hundred times.

"Now get your ingredients and warm up your oven," said Chef Monty.

"And always remember: A happy baker bakes a happy pie."

"I'm happy," said Jacob as he opened the refrigerator door. There on the shelf he saw a bowl of cut-up juicy peaches. "Perfect for a peach pie!" he said.

Jacob slipped into his baking shoes. He tied his baking apron around his waist and put on his baking hat. With one quick flick of his wrist, Jacob turned on his Easy-On Oven that his parents got him because they knew he loved to bake.

"Easy so far," said Jacob as he flung open a cabinet. Inside he found some flour, some sugar, and two kinds of spices: cinnamon and nutmeg.

"Don't forget the pie dough," he told himself, heading back to the refrigerator. "My very first pie will be the happiest pie ever!"

But just as Jacob got ready to bake, Charlotte, his big sister, appeared in the kitchen. "It's time to stop baking and get ready to go," she said.

"Go where?" asked Jacob, reaching for the measuring cups.

"Out to Alfredo's," said Charlotte, "to celebrate Mom and Dad's anniversary."

"What about my pie?" asked Jacob.

"Your pie is not invited," said Charlotte. "But *you* are."

    While Charlotte changed into her celebration clothes, Jacob
remembered one of Chef Monty's rules: Concentrate on what you're
doing—no matter what.

    So Jacob kept on baking. He scooped out some flour and sugar,
and added the two spices.

    "I love to bake!" he said, mixing everything together.

Soon Charlotte was back. "I'm going to read one more chapter while you're getting ready," she said. "Okay?"

"Okay," said Jacob as he sprinkled the sugar mixture over the peaches.

Sprinkle! Splash! Stir! Sing!

"Roll, roll, roll your dough!" Jacob sang.

Jacob used his rolling pin to smooth out all the bumps in the pie crust.
But he rolled so hard that the dough broke apart. Now he had three small
pieces instead of one big piece. "Oh, no," said Jacob. Then he remembered
another one of Chef Monty's rules: If something unexpected happens, fix it
as best as you can.

"Hmmm," said Jacob. "I'll just pinch these pieces together . . . like this."

"Are you kids ready?" called Jacob's parents.

"Almost!" answered Charlotte, turning the page.

"Almost!" answered Jacob, patting down the dough to fit the pan.

Pat! Snip! Cut! Trim!

Next he spooned in the peaches. "Whoops!" said Jacob as some of the peaches sloshed over the top. "Chef Monty says: Always leave your kitchen the way you found it." So Jacob mopped up the mess.

Then he covered the peaches gently with the other half of the dough. Just like a blanket, he thought.

"This is kind of how Chef Monty flutes the sides of his pie," said Jacob as he pressed down along the edges. Jacob pretended the lines were train tracks and his fork was a train. "Toot! Toot!" he said.

"What did you say?" asked Charlotte, looking up from her book.

"Now all I have to do is poke four teeny holes in the top to let the steam escape while it bakes," said Jacob.

Jacob couldn't find a toothpick, so he used his littlest finger.

Poke! Push! Big! Bigger!

Jacob's four teeny holes turned into four giant craters. Just like the ones on the moon. "This pie business is harder than I thought," he worried out loud.

But only for a second, because Jacob remembered another one of Chef Monty's rules: Don't give up, even when what you're making doesn't look the way it's supposed to.

"Are you kids ready?" called Jacob's parents.

"Almost!" answered Charlotte, turning another page.

"Almost!" answered Jacob, setting the pie timer.

Jacob opened the Easy-On Oven door with one hand and balanced his pie in the other. But the floor was slippery.

Oh no!

Jump! Up! Quick! Catch!
"Good work, Charlotte," said Jacob. "Chef Monty says: A baker
can always use a little help. Thank you."

Jacob took his pie and popped it in the oven.
"Good luck, little pie," he said. Then he sang,

> "Pat a pie, pat a pie, baker's man.
> Bake me a pie, as fast as you can.
> Pat it and poke it, and mark it with P,
> And put it in the oven for me, me, me."

"What's the P for?" asked Charlotte.
"For Pie," said Jacob. "What else?"

While the pie was baking, Jacob's parents peeked into the kitchen.

"Ready to go to Alfredo's?" they asked.

"Ready!" said Charlotte.

But Jacob said, "Not yet. I'm still baking." Then he added, "Chef Monty says: Always finish what you start."

No one could argue with that.

Jacob's pie hummed in the oven. Jacob hummed, too. The pale white dough turned flaky and golden. The peaches bubbled, and hot steam escaped through the four holes in the top.

"I'm starving," said Charlotte.

"That pie of yours sure smells ready," said Jacob's parents.

But Jacob said, "Every baker knows: A pie is ready when it's ready, and not one minute before."

Then Jacob sat down and waited like a hen on top of an egg.
Charlotte waited. Their parents waited, too.
Wait! Watch! Wiggle! Worry!

After a while, there was a loud DING!
"Done!" said Jacob.
"Hooray!" cheered Charlotte.
"Finally!" sighed their parents.
"I can't wait to taste it," Jacob said. "But first it has to cool."

Only this time his mother said, "No! Absolutely not! There is positively no time for cooling."

And his father said, "We have to go. Right. Now."

Jacob scratched his head. Chef Monty had never said anything about how to make a pie cool faster.

So Jacob tried some things of his own.
Blow! Fan! Spin! Touch!

But even after all that, Jacob's pie was still too hot to eat.
Jacob sat down. He thought. He thought harder.
Then, all of a sudden, he laughed. "It really *is* as easy as pie!"

First Jacob got out four plates and four spoons.
Next he divided his pie into four pieces.
Then, with a sweep and a flourish, Jacob slid a round ball
of very cold ice cream on top of each piece.

"Now hear this!" he proclaimed. "Chef Jacob's first rule of baking: It's no fun eating a fresh pie all by yourself."

Then he sang . . .

P is for Pie AND P is for PEACH,

Jacob's family ate every last crumb and every last peach of Jacob's very first pie.

"I can't believe we had dessert before dinner," said Jacob's mother.

"It was delicious!" said Jacob's father.

"As good as my book," said Charlotte.

"Thank you!" said Jacob, taking off his chef's hat to bow.

On the way to Alfredo's, Jacob thought of another rule.
"Chef Monty says that a happy baker bakes a happy pie," he said.
"But Chef Jacob says: A happy pie eater makes a baker happy!

"Next time, I think I'll try cherry."

Chef Jacob's Peach Pie

Shopping List

Cherries for pie

Love to Melanie, who got Jacob's first pie started—
and mine too   —C.B.

With special thanks to Melanie Kroupa, who was a
peach to work with on this book   —M.S.

Distributed in Canada by D&M Publishers, Inc.
Color separations by Embassy Graphics Ltd.
Printed in October 2009 in China by SNP Leefung Printers Ltd.,
Dongguan City, Guangdong Province
Designed by Jaclyn Sinquett
First edition, 2010
1 3 5 7 9 10 8 6 4 2

www.fsgkidsbooks.com

Library of Congress Cataloging-in-Publication Data
Best, Cari.
    Easy as pie / Cari Best ; pictures by Melissa Sweet.— 1st ed.
      p.   cm.
    Summary: Jacob watches his favorite television show, "Baking with Chef Monty,"
and bakes a beautiful peach pie, which he gives to his parents for their anniversary.
    ISBN: 978-0-374-39929-0
    [1. Pies—Fiction. 2. Baking—Fiction.] I. Sweet, Melissa, ill. II. Title.

PZ7.B46579 Eas 2010
[E]—dc22
                                                              2008016803

Chef Monty's Baking Rules

A happy baker bakes a happy pie.

Concentrate on what you're doing—no matter what.

If you... best as

...and it.

...king

...to.

Chef Jacob's Baking Rules

- It's no fun eating a fresh pie all by yourself.

- A happy pie eater makes a bAker happy!